Rhino! There's a Rhino in the jungle!"

"Hello, Rhino!"

And Hippo turned
right around.
"That's no Dino,"
he said.

"That's a . . .

Hippo stopped.

Hippo looked.

surprise!"

said Hippo. "I love a surprise! Let's see who is making all that ruckus."

Then those jittery animals stepped back while Hippo walked alone into the tall leaves.

Then that hippo heard the leaves crunching. He saw the mango trees shake.

"It's a . . .

"You four should know better," said Hippo. "There aren't any dinosaurs in the jungle!"

"So you say!" panted Tiger. "But listen . . . listen!"

Dino in the jungle! Run away!"

And they skittered right
into the hippo's mud puddle.

"There's a

"**Dinosaur!**"

yelled Monkey, Parrot, Giraffe, and Tiger.

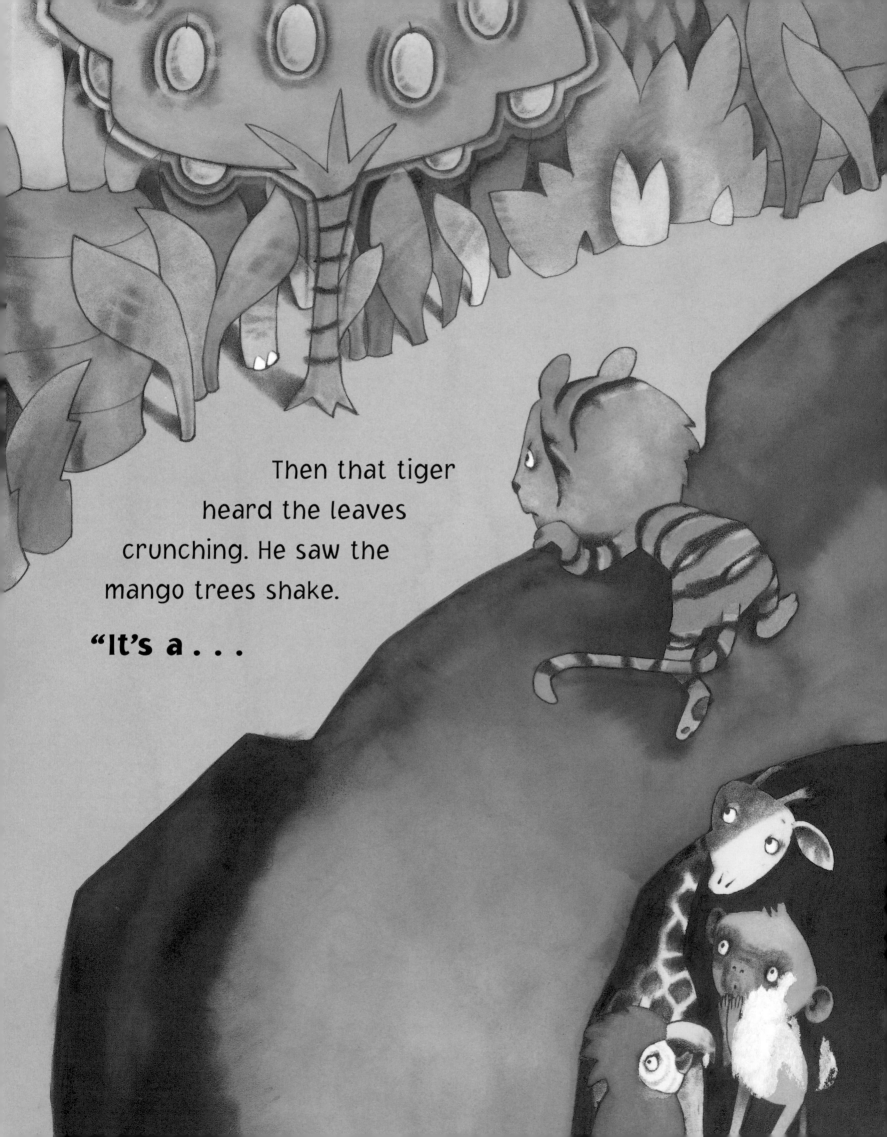

Then that tiger heard the leaves crunching. He saw the mango trees shake.

"It's a . . .

"You three should know better," said Tiger. "There aren't any dinosaurs in the jungle!"

"...ou say!" cried Giraffe.

"But listen . . . listen!"

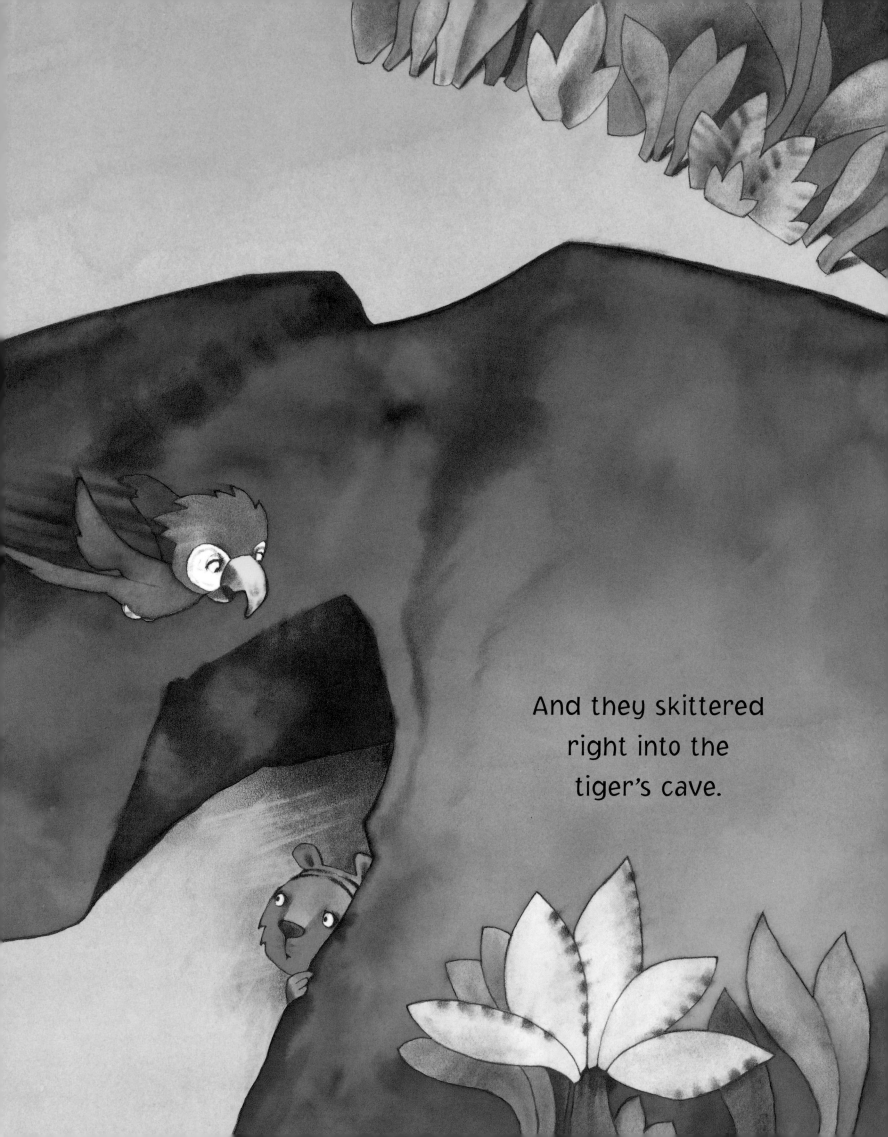

And they skittered
right into the
tiger's cave.

Then that giraffe heard
the leaves crunching. He
saw the mango trees shake.

"It's a . . .

"You two should know better," said Giraffe.
"There aren't any dinosaurs in the jungle!"
"So you say!" shouted Parrot.
"But listen . . . listen!"

And they skittered
right into the
giraffe's meadow.

"**Dinosaur!**"
yelled Parrot and Monkey.
"There's a **Dino**
in the jungle!
Run away!"

Then that parrot heard
the leaves crunching.
He saw the mango
trees shake.

"It's a . . .

"Monkey, you should know better. There aren't any dinosaurs in the jungle," said Parrot.
"So you say!" yelled Monkey.
"But listen . . . listen!"

Dinosaur!"

cried the monkey.

"There's a **Dino** in the jungle!"

And he ran so fast he skittered

straight into the parrot's tree.

One day, Monkey was swinging all across the jungle.
Suddenly, he stopped. Something tremendous was
coming his way. He heard the leaves crunching.
He saw the mango trees shake.

"It's a . . .

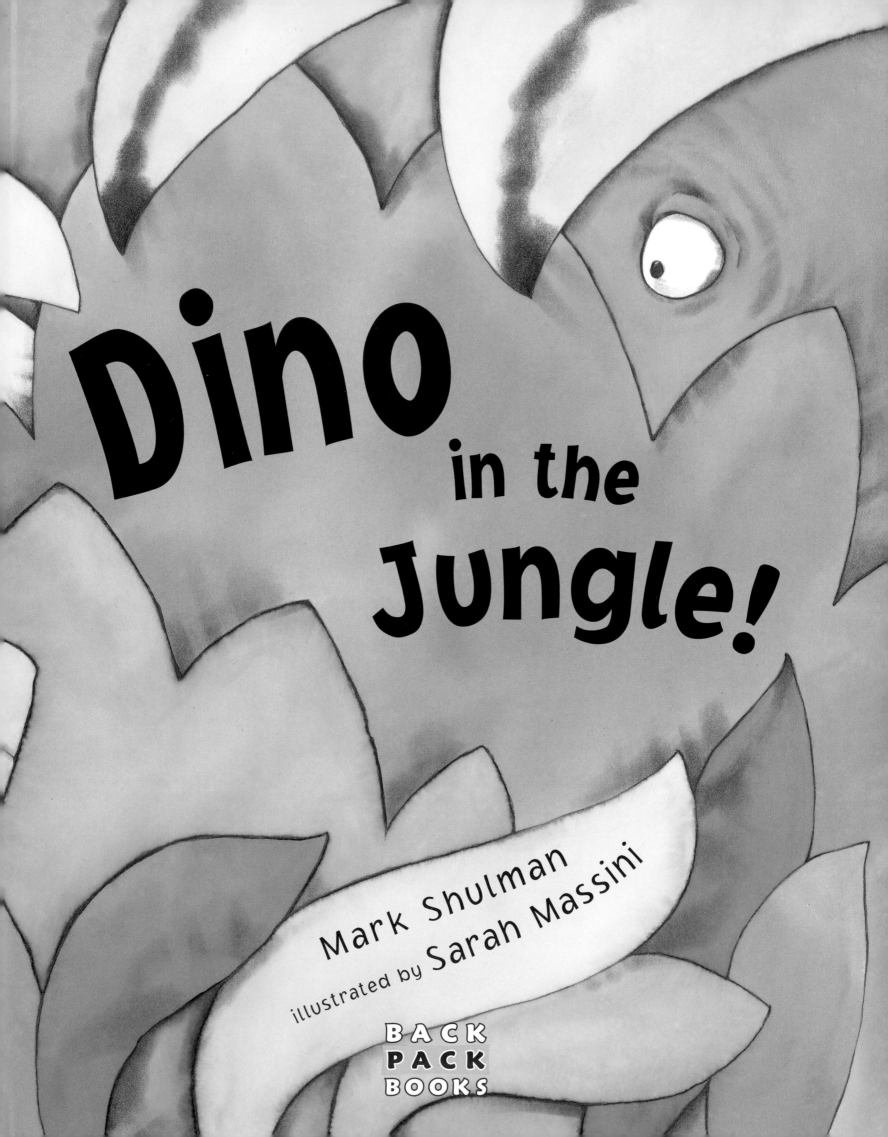

Dino in the Jungle!

Mark Shulman

illustrated by Sarah Massini

BACK PACK BOOKS

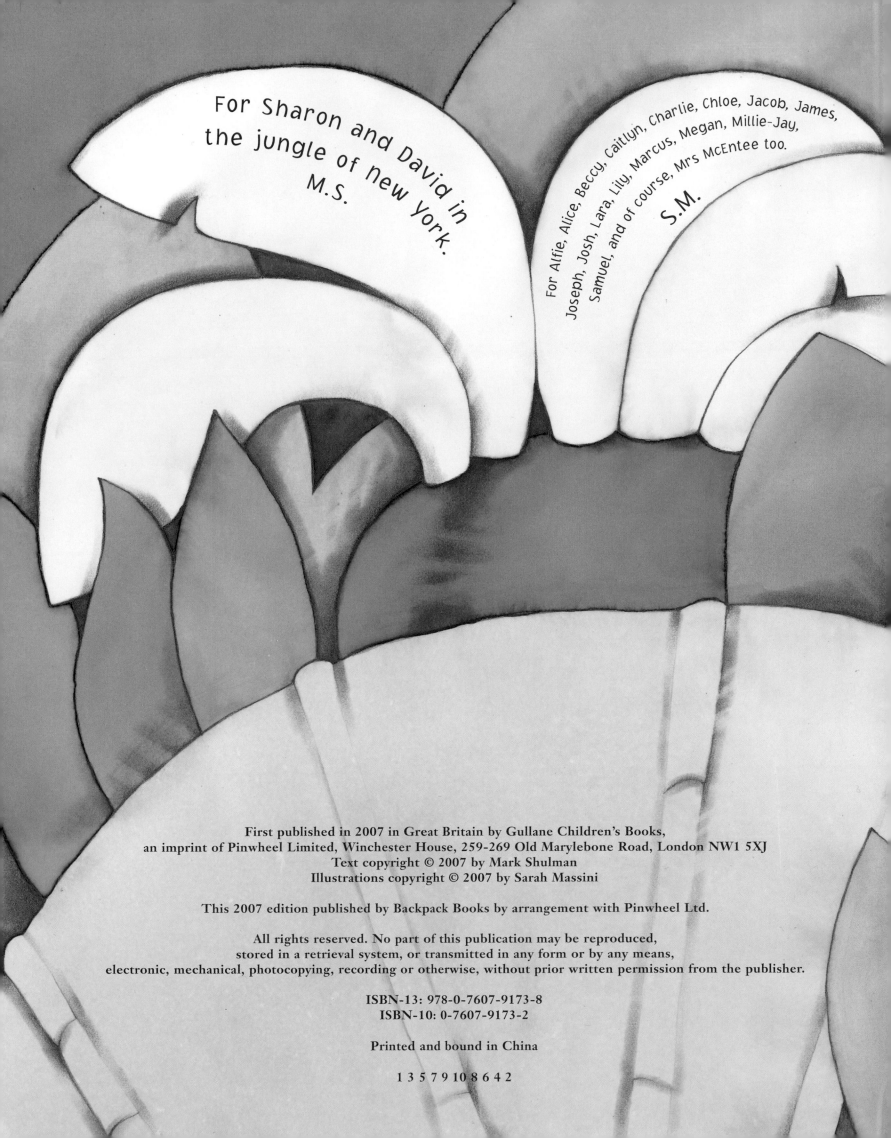

For Sharon and David in the jungle of new York.
M.S.

For Alfie, Alice, Beccy, Caitlyn, Charlie, Chloe, Jacob, James, Joseph, Josh, Lara, Lily, Marcus, Megan, Millie-Jay, Samuel, and of course, Mrs McEntee too.
S.M.

First published in 2007 in Great Britain by Gullane Children's Books,
an imprint of Pinwheel Limited, Winchester House, 259-269 Old Marylebone Road, London NW1 5XJ
Text copyright © 2007 by Mark Shulman
Illustrations copyright © 2007 by Sarah Massini

This 2007 edition published by Backpack Books by arrangement with Pinwheel Ltd.

ISBN-13: 978-0-7607-9173-8
ISBN-10: 0-7607-9173-2

Printed and bound in China

1 3 5 7 9 10 8 6 4 2